Hypocrites

By

Jacey K Dew

Anna Dale

Rules Are Life

Follow the rules to a T, as every rule will help get you through life unscathed.

It all started with a phone call about a month after my eighteen birthday. A newly graduated valedictorian, President of the Student Council, and highest achievement of just about everything academic.

Never partied. Never disobeyed my parents, because I didn't want to; and, partially because I was scared to.

A child my parents were proud and quick to brag about; they did so often.

Nose deep in whatever encyclopedia article I had flipped to, when my cordless phone rang to alert me that someone was calling.

Taking it off the receiver, I answer to a deep voice unlike my Aunt's normally light twinkling one. She notified me that my parents had passed away. They crashed on the side of the road. Their vehicle veered off and flipped into a ditch.

Alcohol was a factor. They believed my father passed out at the wheel.

The phone dropped from my ear at that moment. I never did hear the rest of what she had been saying to me.

The next month was a blur.

I know I cried a lot for the first week. Never in front of people; always keep that stuff private. My Aunt Jann took care of all the legal stuff; with my signing things here and there.

There was a constant flow of people I knew and barely knew; even a few people that I'd never seen before in my whole life. I thought I knew everyone in my parents' life, but I guess I was wrong.

Everyone in town was there for the funeral; at the only church in town. They brought flowers, cards with their name and amount of money they donated in my parents' honour, and food. There was a lot of lasagna; apparently when someone dies you should bring lasagna or a casserole.

Most people brought lasagna. Enough to last six months after their deaths.

It did help though; the ones I hadn't burned. I didn't really know how to cook; not that I ever wanted to learn.

There was no reason to; I convinced myself.

2

My mom did everything for me. I didn't need to learn it, not until I had a husband to take care of; was my reasoning.

Then, it started getting old. 'Oh, Anna. Oh sweetie. You poor thing. I'm so sorry. How are you doing?' They would say.

I got that hang of it after about fifteen of the same conversations, and was able to carefully construct my answers. 'Well, you know. I'm just taking it one day at a time.'

People don't want to hear that you're doing well. My parents died, and I'm living my life because life goes on. Going out for coffee, watching movies, and laughing at things I read.

People don't want to hear that you're doing badly; that you're lost, and have no idea what to do. That you just want to scream, and cry about how it wasn't fair. This wasn't in the plan. That your whole world exploded around you and you would give anything in the world to have those people back.

A mixed bag of emotions at different times. Everyone grieves differently at different stages.

You always give them the constructed answer, and they would just respond. 'Oh, of course. If you need someone to talk to just give me a call. You can come over whenever you like.'

Then I would smile and tell them, 'I will.'

Even with no intention to do so. Then I'd say, 'Thank you, but I have to get going. Have a great day.' And, I would find whatever excuse to leave the awkward situation.

Was something wrong with me?

No, not at all.

It was how I had been taught. It was how I was raised. Be considerate to others even to you own expense.

I knew no other way.

There's a guideline to how you should act in every situation. Follow a strict set of rules and guidelines for everything; to survive life.

My parents loved to have rules and guidelines to life. You follow these rules you will live a long and happy life. I was the poster child for following the rules, since it was so ingrained into me.

Too bad these rules and guidelines don't actually work all the time in real world. They don't work for everyone and every situation.

Not to mention the rules my parents set seemed to leave a lot out. They also gave no wiggle room.

Eighteen and legally an adult. And, I didn't have a clue.

Rule #1

Always pay with a credit card.

"We have to sell the house." I stare at my hand while trying to process what she's telling me.

My parents have been dead a month, and she's telling me that I'm going to have to sell my house.

Part of my parents' legacy was to leave me with nothing.

I'm smart. I took accounting in school, but simple math is all that's needed to figure out that she's right.

My parents didn't have anything for savings, half their mortgage left and no life insurance.

We don't even actually own any of the big ticket items in our possession. We lease the boat, mom's car, dad's truck, and even the car they so-called bought me for my eighteenth birthday. Furniture and electronics were bought on 'buy now pay later' schemes.

Twenty out of twenty two of the credit cards, sitting in a pile in front of me, are maxed out; each has between one thousand to ten thousand dollars maximum limit.

Between the minimum due payments, and all the other bills, my parents had to make a minimum of three thousand five hundred dollars a month to keep on top of things. That's not counting anything like gas, or food.

To sell the house fast, we will probably have to compromise on a lower price than what it is worth. The house owes one hundred sixty thousand dollars to the bank.

All of this gets jumbled into the estate account, and I get anything remaining; if anything does remain.

I won't inherit any debt since my name and signature isn't on anything, thank God, but I might not inherit anything but minor possessions.

My Aunt Jann will return all the vehicles over the next week, or their companies might come to take them back; whichever happens first. They will file with the estate to try to get back whatever they are owed.

I've been rehearsed on what to say when collections call looking for money. That my parents are dead and they have to either write off the debt or try to collect with the estate. If we have a leased item, then they are welcome to repossess it.

My Aunt Jann has the luxury of calling all the credit card companies to tell them of the card holders' passing.

She doesn't stick around after telling me all this news. I don't blame her. I just sit at the table, and stare at the bills and calculations.

Not processing the scribbles in front of me. Anger and disbelief swelters.

How could my parents do this to me? I have University starting in September. The payment is due in a few weeks for the first semester, and the text books. Now, I have to find a job, and a place to live, and a vehicle.

I have to completely start from scratch.

Where do I start?

A job, I need a job paying me before I figure out budgets. I'll need to make a resume. I can talk to friends to see if they can get me a job at their works.

While I'm on it, call people to see if they want to move with me or move me in. That would cut costs. I can't be too picky at this point.

Flipping through our phone contacts book, I land on my contact list and locate anyone that might potentially move out with me. There aren't a lot.

I call out to each person and leave them a message on their machines. Jennifer, Alexandra, and Sheila receive the same message. "Hey, it's Anna. Are you looking for a roommate? I need a place ASAP. Please, let me know either way. Thanks. Bye."

Now, for the job. This time, when I go through the list, I'm less discriminatory about who I include. I'm smart. I can work just about anywhere.

I include just about everyone on my contact list, thirteen people.

Each time, I call out, "Hey, it's Anna. Do you know if your work is hiring? I need a job ASAP. Please, let me know. Thanks. Bye." I hang up.

I go through my parents' contact list next. The list is organized throughout the book alphabetically.

While my list is one page with a name and a phone number, their contacts are full of contact information, birthdays, and addresses for all the relatives, friends, and important people in their lives.

Picking out a dozen and a half people from the book, I phone to inquire about a job. A tailored message is left for people who don't answer.

About half of the people do answer their phones; more than I thought would during this hour.

Some politely decline, others say they'll check, while more say to drop off a resume with their work but can't guarantee anything.

I stare at the phone. Someone's bound to call me back immediately, right? I sit frozen; like this is the only thing in the world that matters at this moment.

I can't imagine being able to find a place on my own. My Aunt Jann didn't offer up her own place, for good reason. She doesn't have the room and I don't think her husband would approve.

Then, finally, the calls and messages start pouring in.

"No sorry." Alexandra replies to both inquiries.

"Not right now, try again in a month?" Cara calls to decline about the work request.

"Sorry no. But, if you give me your resume, I'll give it to my boss. Put in a good word for you." Sheila helps with one thing.

"Let me ask Dean." Jennifer calls me.

Why would she do that? There's hope there now. She's probably with him right now and asking him the question as she's telling me that she'll ask him. Why not just wait the extra few moments to tell me yes or no?

The phone rests on my shoulder, pressed against my ear. I hear mumbling, but can't make anything out.

My ear gets clammy by the time I hear her voice again. "You pay one third of everything and you sleep on the couch. It's a one bedroom apartment, so there isn't much room."

"Yes." I shoot back immediately. Seeing as the others already said no, this is looking like it's my only option. And, it's only temporary right? "If you guys don't mind; I don't mind. Yes. That works great for me."

The questions start in with my having to explain what's happened. Then, we work out an agreement to what will happen for move in and house rules.

"Great. We can make a trip on Saturday to get your things. Noon work?"

"Sure." This is all happening faster than I thought. I don't even know when I have to be out by. It could be a week, or it could be a month.

"Oh and have five hundred cash for then. First month's rent and fees." Jennifer explains.

Five hundred dollars, the agreed sum I would pay each month. It covers my third of the rent, and my portion of utilities and groceries. A set sum to make it easy.

"I will. Thanks." We hang up the phones after our goodbyes.

Great, now where do I get the five hundred dollars from? I have about one hundred dollars in the bank. Maybe some purses have some change and bills.

I do something I haven't done in weeks; go into my parents' bedroom.

I open the door and let myself in. The air is thick and suffocating.

It still feels like I'm going to get in trouble for going into my parents room without their permission. I'm sure the feeling will get worse when I start to go through some of their things.

If I were my parents, where would I stash money?

I check my mom's vanity. There's a change jar on there, but I don't think it has more than just pocket change. It has a quarter and three pennies when I check it. Great.

This is ridiculous.

My parents had thousands of dollars of debt on credit cards, and nothing in their bank accounts.

Why would I think that they might have four hundred dollars' worth of cash in their bedroom?

I'm getting out of here. I go halfway down the hallway, and into my room. I fall back onto my mattress in a huff. This is what my life's turned into.

I'm losing everything, and moving onto a couch. I could take maybe my dresser, though probably not.

Luggage bags then? I could take a suitcase of clothes, and maybe a couple of keepsake items.

I look around my room and at all the things I've collected over the years.

A month or two ago, if you asked me to get rid of a few things I would have been able to part with, maybe, a garbage bag full. Now, I can take maybe a garbage bag full with me; out of this entire house.

What won't fit into a corner of a living room, will have to be sold, donated, or trashed.

My whole life is to be condensed into a suitcase.

Putting that into perspective, then I guess, I don't need much of anything that's in here.

Whimful determination picks me up. I'll have a garage sale.

The desktop computer in the kitchen helps me print off flyers for distribution, and price tags I'll tape to items. I make a full informational poster, with some key items I think might be big sellers and generalizations about what I'm selling. I put the house phone number, and address on them too. Open from today to Saturday morning; at all daytime hours. My name listed for inquiries.

First thing's first, I take the flyers out with me for a ride around the neighbourhood, to the town bulletin board, and on random light poles.

Maybe this will stir up some buyers.

I return home.

Setting to work, I pull up the large door.

The garage is relatively empty.

An argument my parents had over who had the rights to the single car garage, with all the vehicles and schedules, led to a resounding no one gets to use the garage.

Mom and dad's vehicles are parked side by side in the small driveway, while my car is parked on the road.

Dad's tools and equipment litter the walls. I'll sell those too. Make a paper that says to make an offer.

I'll accept anything. No doubt, they'll be getting it for a steal of a deal; I have no idea what anything is actually worth.

What money I can get from anything, is more than I would get if I donate or trash anything.

I have half a mind to just leave anything I don't sell, or can't take with me, in the house for the new people to deal with. The mountain of possessions is overwhelming.

They're all just useless objects now.

I lug things out to the garage. The furniture is too big for me to move by myself. I'll leave that for personal house tours, if anyone is interested. I'll keep in mind to mention it to everyone.

All else is lugged out to the garage and lain out on the floor. I take things out in an improvised order of easy and desirable.

Taking out a fairy to the garage, there is someone inside.

"Anna?" I nod. "Is this the garage sale?"

"Hi, yes. Yes, it is." I confirm.

"I saw one of your posters. There's no sign up front, but the garage door was open." The tall man explains.

"Oh, I forgot to put up a sign on the lawn, sorry."

"Just setting up?" He asks, making small talk as he looks around with a sway of his head.

"Yeah, I've been given a short notice move, so everything has to go."

"How many fairies do you have?" He motions to the one in my arms.

"I don't know. Maybe thirty." I roughly estimate. "I've been collecting them for years."

"Are you selling all of them?"

"Yes. Did you want to see them?" Normally, I wouldn't invite a complete stranger into my house, but this is an extenuating circumstance. "I haven't gotten a chance to get more than five of them into the garage, yet. The rest are inside." My chin motions to the portion of floor where they lay.

He gazes at the ones on the ground, and then follows me inside to my bedroom.

"How much to buy the whole collection?" I have to think about it for a moment. Does that mean he wants to buy the whole fairy collection? I think he might.

I think out loud. "Small fairies at twenty dollars apiece. Fifty dollars for the large one."

"You want them gone right? That sounds like retail price, not garage sale price." He doesn't skip a beat. "I'll give you two hundred dollars to take all of them off your hands."

It feels like I'm getting robbed. The collection

prices into the thousands for what, I'm sure, my parents and I had paid for them. But, I don't have much room for argument.

"Three hundred?" I try to bargain.

"Two- fifty." He counters.

"Deal."

"They're not stolen are they?" His question takes me aback. I am almost offended, but I guess it's always a possibility.

I try to appease his fears. "No, of course not. It's a sob story that I won't bother you with. But, it basically ends in me having to move out and get rid of everything."

He pulls out his wallet and hands me a stack of bills. "Okay. Here's the money. Count it out. It all should be there. I'll take a couple of these to my truck. He picks up the biggest fairy and does as he said.

He seems nice enough and fairly trustworthy. I calm down a bit, and count out the money. It's all there. He comes back to grab another and take it to his truck. I help him load them all up.

His name is Chris, I find out. The fairies are for his partner. He collects them.

We drape a blanket over them in hopes that it will help keep them steady enough to survive the trip.

"Nice doing business with you." He shouts as he shuts the back gate. He hops back into his truck and drives off.

He basically just made off with steal of the deal. Retail, I bought it, or it was given to me for a lot more than three hundred dollars. They cost between twenty to sixty dollars a piece. The large ones were around a hundred dollars.

But, when you need money fast you can't really wait for the right buyer to come along and pay full price.

Nevertheless, it will help out. That's three hundred and fifty dollars now. I only need a hundred and fifty dollars for the rest of the first month's rent.

Whatever else sells should get me to that point and beyond. I hope for extra money, something to buffer between my moving in and getting a job.

I finish the afternoon and early evening with pulling things out to the garage. A few people come by, but leave after a quick look.

A bit of the urgency I had, immediately after finding out about everything, has dimmed a little. I guess I need to pack everything I need for Saturday away.

I close the garage door and lock it from the inside.

Back inside the house, I go to my closet. The whole one side of my closet is dedicated to the boxes of all my collectibles. I forgot about them. They certainly should have gone with Chris.

Oh well.

Those display shelves seem empty now. Years' worth of collecting is now gone. I feel antsy now. I want everything to sell fast. I'm anxious for tomorrow and anxious for the weekend.

Moving to pull out the clothes, I realize I have nowhere to put them. I forgot to pull out the suitcases.

We did have a couple suitcases from our vacation last year. I take the largest of each set. It wouldn't take up too much space, would it? I don't know how to narrow it down as is.

The next three hours turn into a fashion show. What fits? What do I always wear? What has too many holes in it to keep? I end up with a suitcase full of clothes to keep, two garbage bags full of clothes to sell or donate, and one bag of clothes to toss. I take the one straight out to the garbage pickup in the back.

I don't know what to pack for the other suitcase. With so many items in my house, how do I choose to keep a bag worth of items?

I should take my makeup, so I set that in the

18

suitcase haphazardly.

Pictures. My photo album goes in next. I go into mom and dad's room, and find mom's photo albums she made from the time after I was conceived to before she died.

I go back into my room and place them in. There's a bunch of photos from around the house. I take them all down, and out of their picture frames. Those get slipped into the album.

Most of the room is already taken up.

My dad's laptop, now my laptop, has its own bag, so I put everything I need in there now. All my other electronics might as well go in there. Walkman and headphones go inside. Batteries too, to operate the Walkman. I will put my phone charger in there Saturday morning.

I start another pile in the living room; things to take with me.

I place the clothes suitcase and the laptop bag back there.

I don't have too much room left. What to take? I have a purple blanket from my mom. It's probably the most sentimental item in this room that I can take with me. My parents gave it to me when I was little.

I can only fit my toiletries in there now. I'll pack the rest of that Saturday morning.

I take a deep breath in and let it out slow. This is one of my last days I'll spend in this house.

The thought is surreal.

I always thought it would be a gradual thing, and certainly not permanent. My parents would be here, and they wouldn't touch my room so it would be perfect for me and my return each weekend.

I get out of my room and walk around.

I think about all the new or relatively new, within the last couple of years, items in our home. How many of these things do we actually financially own?

The couches are new, and the dining set is new; they're financed with the store. We just bought expensive knives two months ago, a rug, everything I got at Christmas and all that gas for our vehicles. We just charged everything to the card.

I even had my own card, basically. It was my mom's but I've had it for the last two years straight. All the things I bought with it; my clothes, room decorations, lunches with friends, and getting my hair and nails done.

How much of that am I now essentially paying for because my parents charged more to the cards than they made?

Angry at the credit cards on the table, I find the scissors from the knife block, which I probably don't financially own either, and sit down on the dining chair.

I pick up my card and cut it in half.

It isn't as easy as I've seen people on TV do it, but it's satisfying. I cut it into dime sized rectangles.

I need more. One card isn't good enough.

The pile on the table disgusts me. Taking the scissors to each one until they are all cut up. Not as small as the first card, but it's still irreparable.

It feels so good to have card confetti. I throw it up into the air and let it glide to the table.

One last satisfaction is found when I toss them all out into the garbage.

I don't ever want to get a house, and I'm good with a junk car until I can afford to pay out a more expensive one.

I don't need a million trinkets that sit collect dust. Those fairies brought me joy when I bought them or got them, but not far beyond that. Most days, they wouldn't even get a thought; let alone a glance.

A thousand clothes with price tags still on them, never used and bought as a peer induced whim.

Useless objects.

They all cost money, and yet were never used.

Money we didn't even have. How wasteful and stupid was that?

I vow to never ever have another credit card again. It's not worth it.

I will never again reach beyond my means. If I can't pay for it immediately, then I shouldn't buy it.

Rule #2

Never leave food on the plate.

"Cheers to the best first six months of living together, ever! To the sale of Anna's house, and to having an extra bit of money left over to pay for this lovely meal. Thank you, Anna." Jennifer toasts.

We clink glasses together and I take a drink of my iced tea. I'm excited for this food and meal.

This is the first time we've been able to sit down to a meal together since our pizza night the day we moved in. All of our schedules conflict, so we don't usually get to spend time together.

Splurging tonight, I've ordered a great feast with two appetizers to share, our main meals, and dessert for the end.

Appetizers arrive right after I finish my second biscuit. Cheese dip, and stuffed mushrooms both dishes look and smell amazing.

Jennifer tells the waiter we don't need anything else, so he leaves.

We divide the mushrooms up onto our plates to cool down. We each grab a tortilla chip and dig into the cheesy dip.

We idle chit chat as we enjoy the food. Updating each other on our lives; work, school, and friends.

Consciously, because I'll be paying for the meal, I feel like I should take a bit more. The same amount as both of them put together. It's not hard as they both seemingly eat about five chips before they stop.

"I'm not going to be able to fit supper if I keep eating." Jennifer says. Dean agrees with her.

I on the other hand have no idea what they're talking about. I've already had more than they have eaten put together.

There's still more food on the table that needs be eaten. We need to finish what's on the plate before we can move onto the next dish.

We can't leave food on the plates. It's wasteful.

I finish up the cheese dip just in time for dishes. I stuff the mushrooms into my mouth to clear the way.

The dishes look amazing.

It looks gigantic in front of me. We each got the same plate of food. Jennifer looks almost sick at her plate. "Are you okay?" I ask.

"Yes, I just don't think I can eat much more. I'm already stuffed." She says as she looks in disgust at her plate.

"Whatever you don't finish I'll eat." Dean jokes. He's got the same full look on his face. "We can just pack up whatever we don't eat."

I start in on my potatoes; got to save the best thing for last. I eat everything they stack on as side dishes first. They are all quite nice, but I'm really excited for the next parts.

All that shrimp, lobster, and crabmeat; deliciously slathered in the garlic butter. I eat them in that order. It takes a bit, but I get through everything on my plate.

Jennifer and Dean are in various stages of eating there's. Mostly, they've started picking at what's left of their food. It doesn't look like Jennifer has even taken one bite. Dean has gobbled down a few crab legs, but stopped there.

The waiter comes by, "are you finished here? Would you like me to pack those up for you?"

Jennifer and Dean both say, "yes." I don't have anything to pack up. The waiter takes the dishes away.

Quickly, he comes right back and sets down a cheesecake in front of me. I forgot we ordered dessert too.

I push it into the middle and grab one of the three dessert spoons. We each tackle our own sections. I still eat more than they do by the end.

I'm absolutely stuffed.

The waiter comes out with the cheque and runs off. I pull it out of the book, a hundred forty five dollar meal and it was amazing. I place eight twenties on the table.

After a big meal, I want nothing more to go home and sleep.

I feel like it's a little hot in here.

We get up to leave, and suddenly I go from uncomfortable to a great need to find a toilet; immediately. I excuse myself, and run off to the bathroom.

I barely make it in the stall and locked, before I can feel everything come back up. I leaned over the toilet and a mess of everything that was in my stomach gets ejected out of me.

Everything.

My forehead breaks out sweat from the exertion. I do what I would normally dread, and touch the toilet seat. It helps with my sickness and aim.

When I finally get my stomach to settle down, I step back up to test myself. I feel a lot better, but my stomach is still upset.

I flush the toilet and go out to the sinks. I grab a towel and wash my face off. The colors are returning back to my face, and it looks like I'll be back to normal as soon as the water dries.

I'm good enough to go. It's like nothing happened. That is as close to being as bulimic as I ever want to get. I would never have an eating disorder.

The sudden epiphany hits me and I physically stumble at the thought.

I do have an eating disorder.

What I do, is not healthy eating habits. Eating until I get sick, whether I throw up or not, is like binging and purging in bulimia.

This isn't the first time I've thrown up or gotten sick from gorging myself.

How did I get an eating disorder without even trying? Don't you have to actually try in order to have an eating disorder? Unless, it's something subconscious; I guess.

Something deeply ingrained in my mind is causing me to eat like this.

This never happened before my parents passed away.

Could I be eating to fill that hole, maybe I am depressed or could it be something else? Maybe, I'll do an internet search when I get home. See what information I can find on the web.

It's a quiet ride home for me. Jennifer and Dean talk between themselves about work stuff and scheduling.

I sit in the back, staring out the window; lost in my thoughts.

What exactly is my issue?

I can't stop eating. I love food.

Is there maybe something medically wrong with me?

Thinking back to it, that thing Jen said during the meal; I'm starting to feel full. I can't remember ever having had that getting full feeling.

I'm either hungry or nothing, or uncomfortably full, or sick from over eating.

Is that it? Or, just a part? Or, is it something else?

The College Twenty was something I had heard about and just brushed off; until I moved out.

The College Twenty is a thing. But, I don't think it only exists because of budget, and convenience like people seem to think. I think it has everything to do with how parents raise children.

You are who your parents raise you. Their influence deeply imbedded in your brain.

Refiguring and reforming eating habits after you move out is an easy slip. Everything is about convenience and your skill level.

It's refiguring and reforming those habits that are really difficult.

Could this just be college Twenty, or both that and something in my head?

How could your weight change so drastically in such a short amount of time? Just by a change of environment. In six months, I've noticed my clothes fitting tighter.

My parents were not small by any meaning, but they weren't quite obese. My mother had diabetes due to her weight too.

I've never been small, but I'm not fat either; I'm average. However, I'm sure if you'd look at one of those charts in school I'd be listed as obese, especially now.

Is it hereditary? Passed down eating habits?

Getting home, I excuse myself to the couch. Excuse myself to the outskirts of socializing so I can do research.

'Why do I overeat?'

The first search shows up a doctor's website for overcompensating and emotional eating. That could be it. It's the top search and a likely reason.

Maybe, I'm thinking too much into this.

Maybe, not.

So now what? I'll just have to make some more conscious efforts to try to think about how much I'm eating. I'll try it at supper tomorrow.

Maybe, I should try that calorie counting thing, or maybe find out exactly what portion sizes are appropriate for different foods. I do remember something about me only supposed to eat meat the size of a deck of cards. I definitely exceed that on a regular basis. But what if, I try that, and then whatever vegetables I want. And I can read the signs of things and see if there are any recommended serving sizes.

'How to have proper eating habits?'

There are so many webpages. Healthy diet tips, healthy eating habits, twenty two steps to develop help healthy eating habits, changing your eating habits, breaking bad eating habits, losing weight, ten tips on how to develop help healthy eating habits, eating habits and behaviors, eating habits to healthy living, healthy eating habits that save you money, eating habits for children, how to live better and eat well.

I click on one that says 'are your eating habits killing you?'

This website seems to be the mother lode of information. So many tabs to click on at the top for groupings of information. I click on the one at the very right of the section. Tips and Tricks.

'Drink one glass of water before every meal.

At least three meals a day, with two snacks a day.

Do not over eat. Eat proper portions. Do not under eat.

Do not eat a late snack. Do not eat within three hours before bed.

Avoid processed foods. Eliminate sugars.

Most of your plate should be full of vegetables.

Eat on the smaller plates.

When eating at a restaurant immediately half the portion the provide you. If you ask nicely, some restaurants will even half the portion for you and bring you both portions one in a to-go box and the other on your plate.

Exercise often. You should be moving for at least an hour a day.

Keep a food and exercise journal.'

There are so many tips. Some that I would have never thought about by myself. I go back to the homepage and click on a portions link.

The very first thing they say is that most people have no idea what portion sizes they should actually be eating.

I scroll down a bit this page has sections and it. One section is a couple of written paragraphs on portion sizes with a link on how to figure out what your daily intake of calories should be.

The second portion is a slideshow of pictures. One hundred calorie portions amongst different foods. There are all kinds of pictures in here. A very small slice of cake, two slices of bread with a small chunk taken out of one of them, a baked potato, a small slice of cheese, a bundle of celery, and three zucchinis. The pictures go on and on. It's hard to believe the size difference of each of these portions.

Going up to the first section and I click on the calorie counter. Looks like everything is ruled by calories, so I guess I'm calorie counting from now on.

I get redirected to a new page. There's something on there about a BMI index calculator, but I don't pay it much attention.

I go straight to filling out any information.

Basically, it asks for my height, weight, and activity level.

5'9", 180 pounds, age 18, female, and light activity.

I press on the enter button and it calculates the information. The website tells me that I should be eating fourteen hundred to sixteen hundred calories per day, and I should be between one hundred twenty five to one hundred sixty eight pounds to be at a healthy weight.

Wow. I'm not even a healthy weight.

I guess it should be expected though. I don't exercise. I eat. A lot.

I go back to the original website and back to the tips and tricks page. I find where I left off and read the next line.

'You do not have to eat everything on your plate.'

The words strike a chord deep in my gut.

That goes against everything I was ever told as a child. You have to eat everything on your plate. There are starving children in Africa that would love to eat your food. We don't waste food in this family.

And, now this website is telling me that I don't have to eat everything on my plate. I think back to today at the restaurant, and I think that might be the root of it. I guess I could have saved some of it and taken it home to eat later. Jennifer and Dean did.

Something so fundamental that I was taught as a kid, that my parents had ingrained into me, is wrong. I can still hear my mom saying 'you are not leaving this table if you don't eat what's left on your plate.'

My parents were wrong.

It seems like such an earth shattering bang, that my parents were wrong in something they taught me from the moment I could feed myself to right before they died.

An eighteen-year-old rule that has a part in causing me to having an eating disorder.

This one rule, to throw it out and teach myself that it is okay to not finish what's on your plate, may just be the thing to allow me to stop getting sick from eating too much, and maybe lose some weight too.

I close my laptop, and lay on my bed. I'm determined now more than ever to change this.

Starting tomorrow, I'm going to try and break this rule.

Rule #3

Never drink alcohol.

"Just one. Please, it could be your Christmas present to me." Jennifer has been working me all day.

'You've never had alcohol!?!' This admonishment is echoed by just about everyone who's found out since I moved out.

Alcohol is so common amongst adults that you're ostracized if you don't; either that or you're everyone's new favorite designated driver. Or, everyone tries to make you drink.

It's never been something I've ever really thought about seriously, or had to think about. No one I hung out with in high school drank, or at least not that they told me.

That's all I ever hear from people about their weekend now. They went to some party or another, drank their faces off, and how much fun it was. I wasn't invited of course because I don't drink; too much of a buzz kill.

Jennifer has made it her mission to me get me to drink alcohol. She partakes a lot, and wants a wine drinking buddy. Dean drinks too. So do most of my friends, maybe even all of them.

I haven't heard a bad story yet. Hilarity and comradery. Throwing up in bathrooms, maybe. Jennifer has a funny story about being drunk and falling out of a taxi.

Could alcohol really be that bad? Maybe, I'll just try one. It's not like one is going to hurt me. Everyone always talks about multiple drinks to even get a buzz.

"Okay fine. I'll-" I don't get to finish my sentence before I get the breath squeezed out of me by an overexcited Jennifer. She detaches and quickly runs away to the kitchen.

"You know, you don't have to if you don't want to right?" Dean, the voice of reason, steps in.

I smile to show him it's okay. "I know. I want to. Been thinking about trying it."

"Anna, come here." Jennifer says from inside the kitchen. I get to the opening in the wall, figuring that is close enough, and get yelled at again. "No! Come around back."

I do as she says. Dean follows behind me. It's cramped in the small kitchen. There are some shots set out on the counter in a line. She puts

36

one in my hand, one in Dean's and another for herself.

She explains, "it's a Porn Star. This is the shot form, but I want to make sure you like it before I make you the drink form. On three, you clink the glass, and you chug. Okay?"

"Okay." I echo. It sounds simple enough.

"One. Two. Three. Cheers." Jennifer and Dean say. On three, I do as she says. First hitting my glass lightly against Jennifer's shot, and then Dean's. Some liquid drips over the edge.

I take a deep breath. And here goes nothing.

Raising the shot to my lips I pour the liquid into my mouth. There's a lot more in there than I thought there would be.

I resist spitting some back into the cup. The small glass is deceptive. The ease that the others down the alcohol is deceptive. It takes a few gulps to get it down.

Then, the sour taste hits me. My face contorts automatically from the sourness. Other than that, it was good. I don't even taste any heat that I've been told alcohol tastes like; I'm not even sure how you taste heat.

"So, how was it?" She looks a bit concerned with the look on my face.

I force my expression back to normal before I

answer her. "Fantastic. A little sour."

She shrieks a little. "I'll add 7 Up; it'll cut some of the sourness off. I'm so glad you like it. Go sit down. I'll make your drink."

I go sit down in my spot at the dining table.

Taking the scissors, I run them through the wrapping paper I have underneath a stuffed teddy bear. I put the scissors down to replace them with five precut pieces of tape; sticking them each to a separate finger on my left hand.

I take up the left and right sides, and wrap them around the bear, and put a piece of tape there to hold them together. I decide to deal with the bottom next.

It's a bit more difficult because of the shape of the bear, but I manage to squeeze the sides in to create triangles with the top and bottom flaps. First the top, I pull down and tape it next to the bottom. Satisfied with the job, I do the same to the top.

When I finish, Jennifer comes in with the drinks. She chose our tallest glasses, and filled them about as high as she could. Of course she did. One drink, but I didn't specify how much one drink actually should equal.

"Thank you." I tell her as she sets it down. "Who was the bear for again?"

Dean says, "my little sister, Kailey."

"Right." I find the tag that has her name on it. I remove the backing, and stick it on the front of the bear.

Kailey was an 'oops baby'; I remember from asking Dean earlier why he was getting his sister a bear. She's three.

I stick the bear under the Christmas tree. There are a lot of presents collecting under there.

Going back to the table, I grab another present from the pile; The Borrowers for Jennifer's mom. There are only a few things left.

Getting a glance, a side eye, at the level of my drink from Jennifer, I take a big swig of it. She smiles and goes back to her workings. I'm glad she's getting such enjoyment out of this. It's really not that big of a deal.

It tastes fine. I feel fine. I feel normal. There's nothing bad about this.

The movie wraps a bit faster than the teddy bear. The solidness of the object lends to my efforts. I find the last Mom tag and stick it on the front of the gift.

I take a few gulps from my drink before I go to the tree and put this one down next to the bear.

I walk back to the table and wait for Dean and Jennifer to finish wrapping the remaining two gifts.

Finishing about half of my drink, I think I finally start feeling something; maybe.

Jennifer pulls out the cards to play a card game. We've played War a few times, and I think I've won almost all of those times.

Jennifer deals out all the cards into three groups. I have some lows and some highs. My crowning glory are the two aces I've been dealt.

There isn't any outside game talk except when there's an offering of another round of drinks. I oblige Jennifer and she comes back with something new for me to drink each time.

I'm pretty sure I've had four different drinks. Although the last two were in similar cans; different flavours I assume but I never did check.

We play until Jennifer gets bored. While we put the cards away, we try to decide what to do.

There seems to be a bit of a fuzzy feeling starting to creep in at the edges of my thoughts, and I think I'm focusing on things more than normal.

"I want to do something; go somewhere and do something." Jennifer slurs a bit on her 's'. She's started getting drunk.

Dean says, "we're too drunk to go anywhere."

"Fine, then I want to do shots." Jennifer pouts a bit until she gets her way how she normally does; she just decides to do it.

It feels like almost no time goes by until Jennifer's calling us to go into the kitchen.

I get up, but immediately figure out that I'm a lot less steady on my feet than I was an hour ago. It doesn't take long but I get used to it. My head feels good, but light.

Dean doesn't follow me. Jennifer and I take a few shots in the kitchen. They all taste good.

Dean walks in at about our fourth shot. "Maybe you should slow down."

"Oh relax. I'm watching her. She hasn't had enough yet." Jennifer tries to assure Dean. It works immediately to assure me. Dean leaves unconvinced.

I'm not sure how long we're in the kitchen for. There are more shots; more than I can count. I can't count the used shots because after we run out Jennifer washes them, so we can reuse them.

She decides we've had enough when she switches her attention to food. "I'm hungry. I want McDonald's. I wish they delivered."

"That would be the most amazing thing right now." I'm immediately dreaming about McDonald's; it's about the biggest craving for food I've ever gotten. I would do just about anything to get McDonald's right now.

Dean walks into the kitchen. "Nachos?" It seems more like a rhetorical question at this point.

"Yes, please." I say. McDonald's would have been great but now my craving has changed to nachos. It's amazing how fast that can happen. I think, though, any food would do it right now.

I thought it was weed that was supposed to make you hungry, not alcohol.

Dean makes his special nachos. It has queso cheese and layers of shredded cheese. It doesn't take long, it never does, but it feels like forever before he takes it out of the oven.

He takes the nacho filled tinfoil off the one cookie sheet to another. It's cool to the touch so he hands it to Jennifer for her to take it to the table. I follow her out there.

The world around me spins and shakes a whole bunch. It's best for me to sit down, I think.

I grab a nacho. It's hot but I only concentrate on the food and gooey greasy oil. It's the most amazingly delicious food I've ever had.

I feel complete when he brings in the salsa and sour cream mixture.

The chips disappear one by one into my mouth. Barely, a memory of my chewing it. I'm pretty sure I eat most of the tray to myself.

That fact hurts more when my stomach realizes it. Add that to the alcohol, and I can feel something rising up. I'm going to throw up.

Despite the alcohol messing up my equilibrium, I seem to be able to jump up, run to the bathroom, lean over the toilet, and throw up everything.

"Shit." I vaguely notice Dean.

I throw up some more. I feel very hot. I guess I have alcohol poisoning.

My hair gets moved back and gets tied into a ponytail. Something cold is pressed against my neck; a damp cloth.

I can't stop throwing up. I don't understand how I can throw up so much; even with how much I did drink and eat.

I hear yelling. Whoever was here left, and is now yelling at my other roommate.

His voice is loud.

Both Jennifer and Dean are yelling loudly, but I can't comprehend what about. My retching is too loud for me to hear them most of the time, when I'm not throwing up it feels like my hearing shuts down.

I finally get a little break when I start dry heaving; bile is the only liquid coming up.

I sit down straight on the floor and lean my head against my arms; elbows on the toilet.

I close my eyes. I'm so tired.

My stomach rises again. I have to throw up again. Leaning a little forward, I just open my mouth and let it out.

The fighting has quietened down.

I feel someone rubbing my back. I didn't notice them there.

"You need to drink some water. Do you think you need to go to the hospital?" It's Dean.

When everything settles I spit into the toilet, and he flushes it down. "I don't think so." I turn to look at him. He's holding a water bottle. I move to grab it, but I am really shaky and some splashes out. Dean holds the water bottle up to my lips, and I take a couple gulps.

The water stays down for only a couple seconds before I start throwing it right back up.

We continue in a mix of throwing up, him forcing me to drink water, and me falling asleep in a hunched position over the toilet until seven am. When I am finally able to keep water down, we try moving me away from the toilet, while I stay in the bathroom.

"I'll be back. You should try food. Get something solid in your stomach. It might help you more than water." Dean says to me before he gets up and goes to, I assume the kitchen.

I grab the water bottle he left. I take a small sip. Then, another. And, another. I wait for a few seconds. Nothing seems to be happening.

I want to get up. Now that I'm not getting as sick, whatever alcohol induced fever I had is breaking, I'm now only realizing exactly how cold this floor is.

Everything is stiff, and sore. I grab onto the toilet and help myself get slowly off the ground. I don't move far, just to the tub edge where Dean's been most of the night.

So far, so good.

"Feeling better?" Dean asks. He's has a plate in hand. My stomach is hungry, but I almost don't want to try the food because I'm weary of throwing up again.

"A bit." I feel sheepish. No one else got sick like I did. I obviously had way too much alcohol, but until that point our night was going great.

I'd like to try again, but next time I won't drink so much. I really, probably, should have gone to the hospital last night. I had alcohol poisoning really bad. But, oh well. Too late now, and I'm just fine now. They only would have pumped my stomach, and that doesn't sounds pleasant at all.

Dean hands me a plate of plain toast. I bite into the dry bread, and chase with water. Waiting just a few minutes to see if my stomach is going to reject it. When the bite stays down, I take a few more bites.

I manage to keep down the half a slice of toast. So, I take a chance on the second half.

After a half hour of nothing, I decide that I would like to leave the bathroom. Exhausted, I tell Dean, "you can go to bed. I think I'll be alright now. I'm going to try to get some sleep."

"Okay. Come and get me if you need anything." He walks off to his bedroom door and sneaks in.

I slowly go to my couch. Laying down makes the room spin. So, I decide that isn't a good idea.

Going to the kitchen, I find the bread and make myself another toast; this time with butter. I'm getting hungrier and hungrier; I guess that's probably a good sign.

I grab another water bottle out of the fridge. Over the next couple of hours everything with my body returns to normal.

Rule #4

Forgive all; life's too short for grudges.

There are only two people left in front of me.

Thank God.

My teeth chatter from the cold. Shivering in a short dress and heels; a coat is too much responsibility and hassle when out dancing.

I'm probably going to get pneumonia from standing out here. I pull out my ID and ten dollars cover from out of my bra. Hopefully, I can shove this at him, and get in faster.

When it's my turn, I do just that. The burly bouncer must mistake my eagerness to get out of the cold for trying to pass off a fake ID, because he spends what feels like forever looking at the ID, and scanning me over.

Finally, he stamps my hand, and gives me back my ID. I rush inside.

There is an instant heat wave as soon as I get out of the entryway, and coat closet.

Their texts had said they were in the right backhand corner.

I don't make it that far before spotting Lisa and two other acquaintances at the bar. The crowd is hard to get through. Every second I utter an apology to deaf ears after I knock into them.

Once at the bar, I touch Lisa on the back. She turns around looking cross, but at near immediate recognition she hugs me in a tight squeeze. Cora sees me and yells at the bartender to make another. Carol hugs me, then hands me one of the shots.

The bartender makes the shot quickly and soon we are all saying 'cheers'. A straight vodka shot gags me.

I pull out a twenty to pay for a round of apple pie shots, and a screwdriver drink for me. I end up having to pull out another twenty to pay for it all. The bartender gives me back a ten and a five.

The shot she returns with is nothing like the apple pie shot I had at the strippers last weekend.

Green Sour Puss and Butter Ripple Schnapps with cinnamon on top is how I remember the recipe. There is certainly no cinnamon on top, and it shouldn't be a variation of red.

The liquid dispersed and clinked goes down bitter and sweet.

Drink in hand; I follow the girls back to the table. There is a bit more, not much more, light over here. From the looks on everyone's faces, I can tell, everyone is already wasted. There is a rush for hugs; whether I know them or not. A couple of them look like they shouldn't even be standing.

Christie hugs me then when she pulls away she puts her hands on both of my shoulders; I'm sure for balance more than anything else. "We missed you." She slurs. "Too bad you couldn't come to my house beforehand for the pre-drinking."

My first question is what pre-drinking at Christie's house? The second is why wasn't I told about this earlier. "Next time I will; I promise." I bite back the 'if I'm invited.'

I sit down and start working on sipping my drink. I've got a long way to go before I'm as drunk as they are.

If, I can catch up. I have my doubts, though I can certainly try.

The conversation, on the other hand, is easy to catch up on. Girl stuff, mostly about hot guys, and evil boys. A contradiction appears between the motive and end game of tonight.

Lisa broke up with her boyfriend of five years by text tonight, because she was bored with him and wanted to cheat on him. She knew it was over and decided to end it.

That action spurred the all-girls night out. Some think she should make tonight all about the girls, and others are determined to get her laid. She is on game with the latter option.

I finish my drink and excuse myself to go get more. I don't have a buzz yet, so I rectify that by downing two shots, and ordering a double vodka slime.

I get back to the girls and sit down.

"I need a smoke." I don't know who says it, but all of the other girls agree; some sort of drunken mob mentality.

Everyone but me, gets up, grabs their purses, and makes a beeline for the door. They know better than to ask me to go with them to inhale second-hand smoke. I made it clear the first time I drank with them.

My phone buzzes. I pull it out of my purse. It's Dean. 'How's it going?'

'Good! Everyone's drunk already. It's entertaining.' I text back. I notice the time, it's 1230. It's only been an hour and a half since Dean dropped me off. Probably spent twenty minutes outside and the rest inside. Obtaining my drink must have taken around a half hour. Time measurement means nothing in a bar. There is only open and last call.

Dean and I text back and forth for a bit. Ten, twenty minutes go by. No one's returned. I text Dean. 'I think I lost the girls.'

I check the smoking area, and return inside to search the entire bar. Not one person from my group can be found. I text Lisa. 'Where are you?'

I think I've been ditched again. Fifth time with this group.

My phone vibrates from in incoming text but, it's not from Lisa. It's from Dean. 'On my way.'

I decide to go to the dance floor for about two songs. Dean should be here by the third; I don't want to have to keep him waiting for me.

Without a barricade of girls to dance with, the boys cling right to me. I get uncomfortable with the random guys grabbing me, and grinding against me, so I detach myself and leave to go outside.

Dean always picks me up across the street at the over flow parking lot, so I decide to wait there.

Across the street, hands grasp my waist, and a hot breath against my ear freeze me in place.

"You got a smoke?" I can smell the alcohol on his breath as he says this.

I lurch forward, pulling myself a safe distance away from his grabbing hands. I turn around and look at him. It's one of the guys I detached from on the dance floor. He must've followed me out.

"No, sorry." I tell him.

He advances towards me. "That's a shame. I always like a good smoke after I fuck."

I try to back away a bit. Thinking quickly I tell him, "my boyfriend's going to be here any second."

"Then I guess we better hurry this up. We wouldn't want him to catch us." He lunges towards me. The force tackles me to the ground. His hand is in my mouth before I can scream. I gag on his fingers.

The harder I tried to escape the higher my dress goes; much to his delight at my helpfulness. The more I fight the further his fingers go.

I can't help it when the contents of my stomach rise up, and around his fingers, and out of my mouth. At the sight and feeling he takes his fingers out of my mouth, and he goes into a straddling position over my knees.

The new position lets me turn around enough

so I don't throw up more on myself.

When I finish, I get a better awareness of my surroundings. Fingers inside my underwear and rough inside me.

Tears pool in my eye sockets then over flow down to my ears. My hands are useless in beating him.

My name.

Footsteps in the crunching snow are coming fast towards me. The weight cementing me to the ground gets up. I hear a body hit the metal of a car near us.

Opening my eyes to a blurry image of a man limp against the car. Dean stands over him with his fists clenched.

"Dean." I cry as he swipes at the body again.

Dean looks to me. Despite having puke in my hair, and on the front of my dress, he rushes over to me. He helps me to a seated position. He kneels down, and hugs me. "Are you okay?"

I can only say, "thank you" quietly, and hug him back. It's of little comfort.

When he lets go, I noticed the man has disappeared. Dean swears when he figures it out and he helps me up. He escorts me to his car.

It's a quiet ride. I stare out the window.

Did he somehow think I wanted to have sex? Did I not do enough to tell him no?

Dean parks, but we aren't home; instead we're in the police parking lot.

"Let's just go home."

"But-" He tries to interject.

I cut him off. "I want to go home. What are the police going to do? He pushed me to the ground, and we can assume he was going to rape me, but he didn't. You can't get DNA from what he did to me. I can sit with the sketch artist to possibly get an image to the public. If I can remember enough to get something that resembles him. Where someone might recognize the guy or a hundred that look similar. For him to say that I wanted it. For it all to get dismissed as a drunken incident. For them to say that he didn't rape me enough for it to be a crime. He gets a warning, and is released. I get reprimanded for drinking and dressing slutty, and bringing something to the police that wasn't a real incident. Take me home!" I sound harsher than I want to be. I'm pretty sure I'm yelling at him just below screaming level.

He looks dejected, but turns the engine on and drives me home without a word. We go inside the apartment. I ignore him as I grab a change of clothes, and go to the bathroom.

54

The moment I close and lock the door, a tear goes down my cheek. When I glimpse myself in the mirror the dam breaks. I manage to strip myself and get into the shower.

I turn the shower on hot; really hot. The water burns where it hits, but the pain is welcome. I just stand there for the longest time. Sanitizing his touch from me.

I feel dirty to my core.

Maybe it will help to get clean on the outside. Five shampoos, one cream rinse, and five times of scrubbing every inch of my skin.

I finally get out of the shower when the hot water turns cold; about one hour later.

I don't feel any cleaner than I did when I came in here. I get dressed in pajamas. I pick up my dirty clothes and quietly leave the bathroom.

Someone is up and in the kitchen, but I ignore them to put my clothes in the dirty hamper.

Dean comes out of the kitchen carrying two mugs. I can see the string from the teabag hanging out. He places them down on the coffee table, and sits down in the middle of the couch. He turns on the TV, and then hit the button on the game controller. The screen goes dark, and then some music plays. He gets a movie going, and made me tea; I think he's trying to babysit me. I'll play along because it might make me feel better.

I sit down in the corner about as far away from him as I can get. I pick up my mug of tea, and get settled.

I almost smile when he grabs the blanket off to the back of the couch, and puts it onto my lap. As a sign of thanks, I unfold it and throw him part of it.

I take a sip of my tea. It's the Sleepy Time Tea. I don't know what's all in it, but I do know there's chamomile. It's supposed to calm you.

I watch the movie. He chose a comedy; probably trying to end the day on a good note.

As the time passes, I slide further down the couch; getting more comfortable.

Dean leans down at one end of the couch, and I lay down at the other. His side keeps my feet warm.

I don't make it to the end of the movie.

In a blink, I'm alone on the couch.

Yelling wakes me up. There's a hushing sound. I pretend to be asleep when I hear Dean and Jennifer in the kitchen arguing quietly.

Dean spent the night on the couch with me, and it doesn't appear Jennifer approves too much.

Anna Dale

"Are you cheating on me?" She says quietly.

"No!" Out of the shock he says this a bit loud. He lowers his voice. "She had a rough night last night, so I made her tea, and we watched a movie. I fell asleep halfway through."

I grimaced at the m-hmm hum she makes. She starts walking towards the door. "I'm going to work." I wait another minute. Dean goes into his bedroom and shuts the door.

I check my phone. Twenty two text notifications await me.

Words of them ditching me, and going to a house party. Lisa and Carol got into a car accident on the ride home. They are fine. Christie texted saying she was sorry that they ditched me. They thought I was with them. That she hopes I'll forgive them.

My first reaction is to immediately agree. To tell her it's no problem and that I look forward to going out with them again.

My parents always told me that you should always forgive. Don't hold grudges because life it too short to hold grudges.

The rule goes along well with the motto 'forgive and forget'.

As a child, with simple problems, this is easy to do. You shouldn't hold grudges because your friend ate the last cookie when you called dibs, or when that boy pulled your hair.

When you're an adult, things change.

The problems become bigger and possibly more dangerous. The people are less likely to change their ways in a short time period.

These girls have shown me time and time again that they don't respect me. Missing invitations and forgetting about me at the bar is just part of it.

No. No, I won't. Not after last night.

I angry text her back a story long text in multiple messages.

'No. I won't. You're not changing. You ditch me every time we go out. I keep forgiving you but you do it again and again.

What happens if I forgive you again? We go out next weekend and you ditch me again.

What if Dean doesn't make it next time?

FYI, I was almost raped. It's not worth it to go there, spend ten minutes with you, and then I get ditched, and call my ride right after getting dropped off.

It's a waste of my time. This time I'm not going to forgive you.'

Rule #5

Always help your friends.

"Good morning sweetie. How are you today?" Jennifer says to me as she comes out of the bathroom. She says this almost every morning.

"Good morning, I'm good. How are you?" I always repeat back to her.

Rather than go to the kitchen to pour herself a bowl of cereal, like she has always done, she comes straight to me. She sits down on the couch, making me move my legs from under my blankets. I hold them up to my chest and wait for her to talk.

Jennifer starts whispering, "I can't pay rent. Would you mind paying my third this month?"

"Of course." My voice comes out before I can think about it. "What happened?"

I start tallying up the numbers in my head. Do I have enough to cover both her and my portions this month? I do, but I really should use that money to buy myself some clothes. Replace the clothing that has gotten holes in it. And, I'll have to forgo going out for some drinks and dinners.

She lunges at me and gives me a tackling hug. Jennifer whispers in my ear, "They cut my hours at work a month ago. I really thought they would've raised it by now but they haven't. I don't have enough money to pay for rent. I really appreciate this and I'll pay you back I promise."

She jumps right off of me, and runs for the kitchen. When Dean comes out from the hallway, I know what must have startled her. She must've heard Dean's door open. She wanted to make it look like she has been getting cereal this whole time.

I get the idea that she doesn't want Dean to know about her money situation. I'll keep my mouth shut about it. It's not my business to get in the middle of their business.

It's almost the end of the month, and I will have to get her the money after work today. I already have my money tucked away, so I'll give that to her if I don't get a chance to get to the bank today.

Jennifer is really thankful to me the next day. I can tell when I have a Timmy's coffee waiting for me when I wake up. It makes me feel good that I was able to help her out this time.

Days pass. We don't really get a chance to be alone before it's time to give Dean the money for rent.

Over the next month, I don't see much of Jennifer. I assume she has gotten more hours at work.

My time is spent more at home. Without the extra money, I can't go out to do anything. I don't mind taking the hit to my social life and sacrificing a few wants for a friend.

I decide that I would talk to her, but I never get a chance.

The same scene of the month earlier happens again and again.

On the third month, Jennifer comes running to me in the morning and whispers to me asking me if she can borrow money for rent again. The same excuse as the last two months.

She promises that she'll have the money to me before the end of the month, because she has been getting more hours. She's just waiting for the paychecks to come in.

This time I go to my hidden compartment and just give her the money then and there. It's become half expected by now. I'll refill it by the end of the week.

Remarkably, Jennifer gives me back five

hundred dollars one week into the next month. It gives me hope that I might see the rest within a month or two.

The token shows me that she cares to pay me back.

By the time the end of the month comes around she's asking me again to borrow rent money. I gladly give it over to her as she's shown me that she can pay it back.

This tango goes on for about six months. I almost can't keep track of how much money she owes me. I'm pretty sure she's up to two thousand five hundred by now.

At the seventh month it gets worse. She doesn't have enough money to pay for her car insurance. That's another one thousand dollars. Plus, the money she can't pay for rent.

By now, I've run out of money on my biweekly paychecks. I have to delve into my savings to help her pay for it.

She's my friend, and I want to help her; I have to help her. You always help a friend when they need it. Time and money mean nothing if you don't have the friends to go with it.

My parent's cardinal rule for me was to always help people where I can. It was something that my parents really admired in me. I would go out of my way all the time to help someone. It didn't matter how it stretched me for time, or money; I would help.

As a kid, it's being sweet. I was 'so considerate' they would say.

You loan a friend ten dollars to get that big thing they wanted. And frankly you didn't care if you got the money back because, more often than not, it was a toy and you got to play with it too.

You spend an evening helping a friend out, and you just have to spend a couple hours less sleeping in the night to get whatever done.

Over time, you learn to need the appraisal; the good feeling inside that you get when you help someone out when you very well could've left them suffer. People are always very thankful.

I pull from the money I have from the sale of the house. I haven't gone through all of that yet; it's meant for my tuition and textbooks.

I'll take it from that. She'll pay me back before next semester. She promises to get me money before the end of the month.

I set the money on the table for her to collect when she gets off work.

I sit on the couch studying for my English course when Dean comes home unexpectedly.

"Hey, what are you doing home?" I'm almost

afraid of the answer. He better not have gotten fired.

I can't support two people.

"I am," cough cough, "sick." He laughs, and then further explains. "I have too many sick days built up, so my boss told me to go home sick."

"They can do that?" Relief hits me. His work must like him to do that; or at least his boss likes him.

"Yeah they can and do. It's use them or lose them, right? So, I might as well take them. I've got tomorrow off too." He walks over to me.

I can smell the gasoline on his clothing. It smells really good. I take in a deep breath. He doesn't walk by me as I expect him to do. "What's with all the money on the table?"

My heart pounds with guilt and panic. I forgot about that. All of the money I am going to lend Jennifer is just sitting on the table. I white lie to him. "It's Jennifer's. It's for her car insurance payment and rent."

"I paid her insurance last week." Dean's caught my lie, but now I've caught Jennifer's.

"What?" I can't help the question that blurts through my mouth. The confusion and meaning hurts my head and chest.

"Yeah, her hours got cut at work. I've been

covering her bills for the last few months." Dean explains. The story is a familiar one that Jennifer had fed me.

I drop the English book into my lap in shock. I stare at him for a moment. "She owes me two thousand five hundred dollars because I've been giving her rent money for the last six months. That's my money and I was going to give it to her because she couldn't pay her rent or her car insurance this month."

I put the book on the table and gather up the money. I put it in my hiding place, and sit back down in a huff. My face is hot in anger.

"Are you serious?" He puts his hands on his face trying to hide the emotions. "She works late tonight. I'll talk to her in the morning. I'll get your money back."

He walks off to go take a shower. I thank him, though, I'm not sure he hears me.

Jennifer doesn't come home before I fall to sleep.

I wake up in the middle of the morning to a slammed door. Dean must've heard it to, because he runs out in nothing more than his boxers.

I grab up the decorative wooden tray from the table. Readying it to bash whoever thought they'd break in to our place.

"Jennifer's gone." Dean informs me.

While Dean runs to the door and out into the hallway, I go to the porch and open the door. I barely get out there before I see Jennifer's vehicle driving off.

Dean comes back in closing the door behind him. "I'm sorry. I'll pay the money back myself."

He starts walking back to the bedroom but I'm still in a daze; mind still half asleep trying to figure what's going on. "What happened?"

"She woke me up when she got home last night. We had a fight, and then went to bed. Her stuff is gone, so I guess this is her telling us that she breaking up with me and that she's moving out. If it's not that, then it's going to be. I can't deal with her anymore." Dean gets up and goes to bed.

When I go to get my rent money a couple of days later, I find out that she had taken the money I was going to lend her, and my money for rent.

We never saw her again. She changed her number; her parents wouldn't tell Dean where she was. They threatened to get a restraining order against him. Cross words and names were thrown at him. We can only imagine what she told her parents about the abrupt breakup.

Four thousand dollars I would never see again. I technically broke up their relationship because I lent Jennifer money. There were many other things that contributed to it, but I was the catalyst.

That wasn't the last time I lent money though. The last time I lent money was to another friend of mine Selene. She needed the money to pay her rent, because she was expecting an expensive radar ticket. I lent her the money, one thousand two hundred dollars, and never saw it again. She didn't pay me back a cent after six months and when I confronted her, she got extremely defensive.

I haven't seen her since.

It's looking at the little things too. After I stopped being friends with Selene I started realizing that I had more money.

After a good look at my bank statement, I found out why. Nine times out of ten when Selene and that group of friends would go out for anything, I would pay for more than just myself. I didn't want to tally it, but month and months of hanging out with them, all stopped when Selene got mad about me asking for my money back.

All my friends stopped hanging out with me, likely because Selene told them to; likely because I refused to pay for anything else. No longer were we going out every Friday night and spending hundreds of dollars of my money.

When you become an adult the stakes are much higher, and you start caring about whether or not you receive anything back. If you don't, you might not eat for the next week. Or worse.

As an adult you're still sweet, you're still considerate, but you also start carrying different names; you then become a people pleaser or a pushover.

As an adult once you're a people pleaser, it's no longer your choice to help people. It becomes expected of you; no matter the cost. People take advantage of you when you become a pushover.

It's about being fair. You loan money to someone, then you expect to get it back. You continually pay for them, and you expect that they will return it with more than a fake friendship.

What's the use of time and money, if that is the only reason why you have friends.

Rule #6

Go to University and get a real job.

I feel like I'm going to be sick.

Sitting outside in the parking lot and dressed in all my best clothes, I'm nervous for my first day of school. This is my first real job.

I'm barely twenty five years old, starting a career that will last me for the rest of my life. And, I'm acting like a teenager hiding out in my car as a nervous wreck.

Finally, I get up the courage to finally go in. I open my door and get out. I close and lock my door and tried to exude confidence as I walk to the school doors from the teacher's parking lot. I stumble a couple times. I should have practiced a little more in my new heels.

It's too late now. I go inside the door and go straight to the office. As soon as I get in, Mr. Wexler comes rushing out from his office. "Are you excited?"

"Very." I don't have much for words as I try to focus on remembering what to do today.

"Relax, the first day of school is just to get to know your students and establish your timeline for the rest of the year. You'll do fine." He puts his hand on my shoulder and squeezes a bit to try to comfort me.

"Thanks. I should probably get to my classroom and start preparing." I back away from him a step. Enough to get out of his grip.

"Of course. Don't let me keep you from it. If you need anything throughout the day just ask." He says, and gives me a reassuring nod.

"Thank you, have a good day." I go to the lunchroom and put my lunch in the fridge. I go back out of the office.

There's no check-in system, you just come right in. Someone sees you and just confirms your there. That's why I made my lunch today. It makes sure that someone sees me and confirms that I am there so that there are no issues.

I'm paranoid that in somehow, some way, I'll get an absence just because no one sees me. It doesn't make sense, of course, because who would then teach my class if the school didn't call in for a sub.

But there's still that paranoia.

My classroom is all the way on the other end of the school, right across from the library. I pull my room keys out of my pocket and unlock the door going inside and leaving the door open behind me. The school has locked doors that only open from the inside, some sort of a security feature.

I turn on the lights. Nothing has changed from when I was here a week ago. It was a long week last week; meeting the entire faculty and setting up my room. I go to my desk and sit down and turn on the computer.

Looking around the classroom, it feels so strange to be in this position. I have never been in this position. I feel like I should be sitting down in one of those dinky little desks meant for my high school students.

High school students. It feels like forever ago that I was a high school student myself. In reality it was only seven years ago.

Half hour until the bell rings. I gave myself a lot of time, so I have nothing to do. I feel like I'm not ready.

I log into my computer and open up the absentee list for my first class; eleventh grade English. I have four classes today and three classes tomorrow. I'll have a spare class right after lunch every second day.

I start to think about what I have to do today; try to go over it in my head.

Introduced myself.

Take attendance.

Play the 'tell me about yourself' game.

Go over the syllabus for the semester.

And, get the students to write something.

Then, they will read aloud in class.

It doesn't seem like a lot, but hopefully it should fill up each short class.

First day of classes are short classes to introduce the students to the teacher and vice versa.

Twenty five minutes until class.

I know I have everything done. I finished everything last week. So what do I do now?

It's a real job. I'm basically in charge myself. So, does that mean that I'll get in trouble if I pull out my cell phone? Can I play games on my computer?

I'm technically on the job now; and getting paid for being here. If I'm getting paid to just sit here, then why can't I play on my phone? Or, should I be finding something work related to do?

Besides playing on my computer might not be a good idea. I don't know if they monitor the computers here.

Not ruling out playing on my phone, I try to figure out something to do just to make work for myself.

I get up from my desk and walk a couple feet to the whiteboard. I might as well put my name down on the board before people get here.

Miss Dale.

That's going to be weird. No one has ever called me Miss Dale before.

Can I have them call me Anna?

No, that would be unprofessional. And, what would happen when the other teachers find out that I let my kids call me by my first name? For something so simple, I don't want to already be the laughingstock. It wouldn't be very good to have my kids disrespect me on the very first day and allow it.

I might be able to make work organizing and reorganizing my classroom. I'm pretty sure it looks just the same, as it did when I got here, by the time the bell rings.

I go down in my chair and anxiously wait for the kids. It doesn't take long for me to be able to spot out the keeners. Someone like I had been.

The kids are always first to class, the kids who are the teacher's pet. They come in with a cheerful greeting and quietly sit down and open their binder to the next page. They pull out a pen and get ready to take notes.

The other students follow shortly after. It's easy to tell that these kids are just getting back from summer vacation.

The next bell rings, signaling that anyone who comes in after this is now officially late. I start worrying with the few empty desks. What do I do? I decided for the first day that I'll let it go but not in the future. I keep the door open. I'm not sure if you're even allowed to close doors now. There's a couple of stragglers who come in and I start the class.

"Welcome to English. My name is Miss Dale and I'm going to be your teacher for this semester." The students start to quiet down. A couple of the students shush the others. But it doesn't really work so I try something else. "Quiet down. I know you're also excited from summer vacation and getting to see friends again, but let me get through this and perhaps you can talk at the end of class. Find your seats and settle down." I accomplish it. They actually listen to what I say. So far, so good. "To start things off we are going to play a little game. Same thing you'll probably do in all your classes today. It's really simple. A get to know each other type game. Tell us something that happened over the summer vacation. I'm going to start. My name is Anna Dale. And, over the summer I got this job and went to Mexico. And over to the girl on the far left. How about you go next?"

My first day goes really well. I'm excited to work with all the students for the following semester.

I go home and share a bottle of wine with Dean. Celebrating my first successful day at my real job.

The next day, I'm not even nervous anymore. I walk straight into the school and go right into my classroom. I figured out that I don't have to be a half hour early; I technically just have to be there by the time my first students get to class. I give myself a five minute buffer and this time I'm excited when the bell rings.

It's the second day of class and you can tell the students are a bit more subdued than the ones yesterday. They've caught up with all of their friends and hopefully are ready to get to work.

I get through half of the classes before any issues arise; second class, half way through.

This class is getting a little more talkative as time goes on. They should be using this as writing time not using the time to talk to friends.

I decide to let them be. I can use this to figure out if this class can still work get their work done and talk at the same time.

It becomes more and more clear as time goes on that they aren't working anymore, so I decide to say something. "You can talk as long as you try to also get your work done at the same time. If you can't multitask, I will have to take away talking privileges." I go back to grading the other class' freestyle writing.

Only a couple minutes later and they are already talking at the same levels. I can see only a couple of people that are working. "This is your second warning. If it wasn't clear the first time, if you don't start working, I will have to take away talking privileges; while you are working, for the rest of the year." A few people take out their books to write down something.

Satisfied, I go back to work again. This time it takes even shorter for people to get rowdy again. "Alright, no talking for the rest of the writing time. I don't want to hear a peep out of you. Go back to your seats, sit down, and start writing." To my surprise they do just what I say. We get to telling our stories before I have another issue.

Jake holds up a piece of paper. I can see there isn't too much on it, but he was one of the talkers, so I'm not surprised. I might have to have a word with him later.

"Mrs. D why don't you chill instead of telling us to be quiet. Why don't you use that pretty little mouth and do something else. Don't be a hard ass and just let me pass. Maybe I'll let you get some in the-"

"Enough!" That did not come out like it should, but I wasn't expecting anything like that. "Jake that is completely inappropriate. I will need a word with you after class."

"Heads up. I got a date with Mrs. D after class. Who knew would be so easy to pass?" The whole class gets a chuckle out of this. I don't know what to do. But he can't say those types of things. Someone may get the wrong idea; will get the wrong idea. "Go to the principal's office." I tell him firmly.

"No thanks Mrs. D, I'm not into three ways; at least not with another guy." I feel like I'm going to cry. I'm getting sexually harassed by a sixteen year old high school student and I've probably lost the respect of this class for the rest of the semester.

Jake finally does leave and I tell the principal he's on his way. After I get off the phone I get back to class.

I decide to pick a couple of students who I figure are the good ones. I don't want something else like that to happen. The rest of class goes okay despite my complete embarrassment. The bell rings and I let my students go.

I get a knock on my door and another teacher lets herself in. I was introduced to her last week but I don't quite remember her name. I do know she's the Gym teacher. "Mr. Wexler wants to see you. I'm taking your next class."

I manage out an, "okay." I get up and leave. I figure it might be something to do with Jake. It might be protocol or something. When I get there, Mr. Wexler shuffles me into his room. Jake isn't there.

He sits behind his desk and folds his hands. "Anna, can you tell me what happened with Jake?"

I explain my story. "The kids did a free writing assignment and Jake's was about me having sex with him to pass."

"I talked it over with Jake and he will never do it again. He apologized and said he meant it as a joke. You're a new teacher and you don't know how to handle the class yet, but we can't let something like this happen again. We don't send students to the office. We're not allowed to take a student out of class; you're prohibiting them from learning."

I'm getting in trouble. I'm getting in trouble when he's the one who sexually harassed me in class.

I don't understand. I don't know what to say.

He goes on further to say. "Take off this class and go for an early lunch. Come back refreshed. Maybe ask some other teachers for tips on how they deal with their students."

I put on a brave face, but I feel like crying. Not until after I'm away from here. I mumble an "okay" and bolt out.

I'm not going back to the classroom and I don't have my car keys. I decide to go for a nice long walk.

I walk out of the school and immediately over to the crosswalk. I cross the road and walk down the block.

By the time I leave the school grounds I'm bawling. I walk far enough away that it would be impossible for anyone in school to see me, and so I can try and find a place to cry alone.

There's an empty park a block away, so I go up to the top of the slide. I sit in there and don't go down. I try to listen for anyone coming, but it's hard to hear over my sobbing.

I got in trouble because I sent a student to the principal's office for making sexual comments towards me.

I got in trouble.

Now I have to deal with this student and this

class for the rest of the semester; every second day for four months. I hope that everything will be okay come Thursday, but I doubt it.

It's high school, and you can't recover from something like this. I know. I've been classes so mean to the teachers that they quit. If I can't handle the students, it doesn't matter how good I am at teaching or how much I love to teach, I'm gone.

Maybe this job just isn't for me.

I spend the next four hours crying.

Eventually, I make my way back to school in time for my last class. Some of my spark is gone and I just want the day to be over.

It was hell, but I finish the day.

Going back the next day is really hard. I have a major hangover from the vodka cure last night to boot, but this is the good class.

I get to my class and start my computer. I go into my teacher's email and see a note from Mr. Wexler.

It's too much to hope that he wants to apologize, but as the subject line is 'The Incident' I can tell he wants to talk about Jake. I can't ignore it however, because if he wants something timely I'd get in more trouble if I ignore it.

80

I click on the email.

Anna;

Jake has been pulled from your class and a formal complaint has been launched against you, by his parents, for embarrassing Jake in front of his classmates. A formal apology is required to Jake and his parents, for them to drop the complaint. You will write the letter or you will have to face suspension, for an indeterminate amount of time, while an investigation is done.

Immediate tears are brought to my eyes. Once again, I am in trouble because of this student and this thing. I believe it should have been handled differently, and it shouldn't be handled this way now.

I had heard about all the stories while I was in university about schools protecting students rather than teachers. But I didn't think it was this bad.

I need this job, so I write up the letter before my students come in and I send it off to Mr. Wexler. No comments made to him.

The end of the day comes after what feels like days. I don't talk to Mr. Wexler for the rest of the day. I go home and crack open the vodka. This is starting to become a trend. Three days into my job and it's making me an alcoholic.

All I've learnt from this situation is these

things: Never let your students talk about what they wrote in free writing. If something happens, I'm just supposed to keep telling the student to stop. No sending the student out into the hall. No sending them to the principal's office because my principal won't help me and won't do anything for me. And, gossip including a student lasts for a day and spreads through a tenth of the student population. Gossip about a teacher spreads to the entire school population and lasts for the rest of the semester.

Now I know why teachers are always so happy, happier than the students, by summer vacation. With a second semester almost just as bad as the first, it makes me wonder if I'll be invited back next year.

I leave the school for the last time this school year. I go home and for the first time in months, I don't immediately crack open an alcohol bottle.

I lay down on the couch and close my eyes. It's so relaxing that I don't even notice Dean come in and just hear his whisper. "You know we got the bigger apartment so that you could have your own room to sleep in, and so you could stop hogging the couch."

I open my eyes and tell him, "I'm not sleeping."

"Kind of surprised not to see the vodka out.

Alchy." I glare at him but not for long, because it's true. Even I can admit I've become an alcoholic this year.

He has something behind his back and when he notices that I am looking there, he pulls out a bottle of wine. He sets it down on the coffee table and goes into the kitchen to pull out two glasses.

"So, what are we celebrating?" I'm curious. Is this about my last day at school?

"I got a promotion. You are now looking at management, and a nice raise to a hundred and fifty thousand dollars per year."

I say, "Congratulations," but I really want to slap him.

In my anger, I down the entire glass of wine and pour another. How is it that Dean has a job where he makes a hundred and fifty thousand dollars in a year, and has no stress, and is completely happy at his job? He loves his job.

Meanwhile, I'm stuck with a thirty four thousand dollar salary job with student loans climbing by the month with interest. I hate my job. I've become an alcoholic because of my job. And, I could go on about my hellish life.

I watch Dean play Fable. My drinks keep coming. I get more and more drunk as the night goes on. I start thinking more and more into it.

Obsessed.

I pull out my phone and start doing calculations.

I make $34000 per year salary. No. Scratch that, I take home $1050 per two weeks. Times 2. Times 12. I take home $25200 per year. I work 7.5 hours a day, plus prep and marking. So I'll say an extra two hours on top of that; during the school year. So, that's probably an average of 9.5. So 9.5 hours a day, 5 days a week, 4 weeks in a month, for 10 months of the year equals 1900 hours. $25200 divided by 1900 hours equals $13.26 per hour. So I technically make $13.26 per hour as take home pay. That's not even four dollars more an hour than what I was getting when I was waitressing.

I would take home $550 every two weeks. If, I didn't work overtime. So that's $1100 per month times 12, so I would bring home $13,200 every year. On the average night I would get $100 in tips, times five nights a week, times 52 weeks in a year equals $24,000. That can't be right. 100×5×4 weeks in the month. Times 12 months in a year equals $24,000. $24,000 in tips per year not taxed.

That's right.

Making my wage as a waitress for take-home pay of $37,200 per year, minus $25200 equals an extra $12,000 a year that I'd make waitressing.

I guess that's why I've had to tighten my belt a lot this year. I thought it was my new alcohol habit.

Anyway, 6 hour days 5 times a week times 52 weeks in a year is 1560 hours. $37,200 divided by 1560 hours equals a technical bring home wage of $23.85.

I put my phone down in frustration.

This is enough. It's disgusting.

I might as well go back to waitressing. You make a hell of a lot more money working at the right place, if you're friendly and don't screw up too much.

Everyone tips nowadays. It's grueling work. The majority of people are nice-ish. The people that you work with are generally friendly and interact with you. You've got a lot more down time when it's not busy, but I still managed to make about a hundred dollars in tips per night.

I still remember that night I came home with five hundred dollars in tips. That's what happens when you wait on a bunch of drunken college guys.

Why did I get a real job?

To rack up forty thousand dollars in student loans, which will probably be sixty thousand dollars by the time I'm done paying it off. To spend four years in the school, when I could have been making more money. How many hours did I stay up because I had to work and go to school the same time? All the stress and the homework. Then, to spend three years trying to get a job in my field of expertise, but failing.

I probably wouldn't have gotten a job in teaching, if I hadn't run into Mr. Wexler.

I should just quit. There is absolutely no use in me keeping this job. An hour drive to work, and an hour back home. Then you have to deal with stupid teenagers all day. The bad definitely outweighs the good.

No matter how good I am at teaching, no matter how much I loved it when I was a student and I had to tutor someone. It's not worth it. Why the hell did I go to a job that I absolutely hate?

And I wonder if this is a common thing? How many people actually have jobs in the field that they studied for and went to school for. College and university; the ones that you have to pay thousands and thousands of dollars for an education. Not only that, but in so many of my University classes I had to teach myself, because the teachers sucked.

I pull over my laptop. Over to Google and I type in 'how many people have jobs they went university or college for?'

Seeing the results, I kind of wish I would have Googled this first, before I went to college and university.

There are so many pages of links and sites. The headlines are various but all carry the same sentiment.

Is college worth it? Why are so many people out of work? 70% of college grads can't find work in their field. 100 reasons not to go to university. The reason new graduates can't get hired. From school to welfare. School is the biggest legal money scam out there.

This is truly disgusting. I look at the websites to make sure that some of these things are legit. Almost everything comes from some sort of credible website; from news sites to business magazines.

I put down my laptop. I guess I have the summer to think about it.

By the time summer ends, I get sucked into teaching again. Thinking, maybe this year will be different.

It wasn't. Neither were the next two years.

Twenty nine years old. I'm too old to be a waitress, I tell myself. What am I going to do? It feels like I've slept away the last few years.

This isn't how anything was supposed to be.

I'm sure my parents are rolling over in their graves. I'm a twenty nine year old woman, living in an apartment with a guy who's not my husband. I'm an alcoholic, and I have no life.

I go over this year, after year, after year. My friends tell me year, after year, after year, if you don't like it just change it.

It's not that easy.

In fact, Dean and I went over this yesterday. I decided I might as well wait for my five year anniversary, and then I can get a job closer. That should help with job prospects. It'll be different elsewhere.

My phone buzzes. I look and see a message from Dean. 'You start tomorrow. No excuses.' What is he talking about?

I text him back, 'Start what?'

He doesn't answer. In fact, he doesn't answer for the rest of the day.

I basically tackle him when I get home. My first words through the door are, "Start what?"

He laughs, and just lightly shoves me away. He walks past me and says over his shoulder. "Your new job. Parts washer for eighteen dollars an hour. Give it a try. If you like it, quit your teaching job. If you don't like it, you can quit, but at least give it a try."

This is a job that my parents would definitely roll over in their graves about. Me, their valedictorian will be washing parts. It's definitely not a nine to five job. In fact, I work seven days on and three days off for twelve hour days.

All it took was a week. One week and I was hooked. I quit my job as a teacher.

I work with a bunch of laid back people. We blast music throughout the warehouse. I no longer come home with the need to pick up a bottle of alcohol. As far as I'm concerned this job is practically heaven.

So much for 'go University, and get a real job.'

It sounds simple, but it's really something you have to work hard to complete by the end of the first quarter of your life; and that's if you live to be a hundred.

One year of preschool, one for kindergarten, six years of elementary school, three in junior high, three more in high school, then a varied amount of years in University; though the average is worth four years.

About eighteen years of schooling to get a real job.

Or, eighteen years of schooling to get a job not in your field, while you desperately try for three years after you graduate to get one.

Only after talking with an old friend of my father's, did I finally get a job as a teacher; an hour drive away.

I did what I was supposed to. Being a teacher was on the approved list of 'real' jobs.

But, I hated it.

Rule #7

No sex before marriage.

I am fully convinced that this is the reason why my first marriage failed; a marriage that only lasted one year. There were other issues of course, but everything comes back to the sex.

I met my husband when I started working as a parts washer. He was one of the other parts washers.

We hit it off, and by Christmas we were engaged. By summer we were married. I was almost a thirty year old virgin, but I missed it by a couple weeks.

On my wedding night I lost my virginity, while also finding out that my husband had been with at least fifty women. I didn't let it bother me, at first, and we had a good night.

The sex was good, but I couldn't help but feel a little cheated. While I saved my virginity for my husband, he definitely did not save his for me.

The second issue, sex was not at all like how it is portrayed everywhere. It was awkward. More so, because he knew exactly what he liked, while I had no idea what I did and didn't like. It took a while for me to be comfortable refusing things I didn't like, while knowing that it was what he preferred.

The third issue came the next day. It was mortifying. I don't think my face was anything other than red for an entire week. Every single person I know knew that I had sex. Every single person knew I had lost my virginity. Something that had been so taboo for my entire life, was suddenly so out in the open. And, no one held back.

This made me so completely conscious about myself that I started closing myself up off from everyone I knew. That meant I was always home and didn't see anyone. I made all the excuses not to go anywhere with anyone.

I started getting cabin fever but I resisted because the embarrassment was bigger.

Then, I stepped on the scale. I had gained ten pounds over the last month.

This made me more self-conscious than I had ever been before. I was determined to lose weight.

I stopped having sex unless it was in complete

darkness and stopped letting him see me naked. Determined to do so, until I lost the weight.

The days between sex lengthened. One week became two weeks, and then it became four. Pretty soon we had not had sex for four months.

My husband felt the need to remind me every second of the day that he was home and anytime we crossed paths at work.

I hadn't lost any of the weight, in fact I had gained another ten pounds; stress weight from stress eating. Uncontrollable eating urges to curb my emotions.

More self-conscious than ever, I didn't want sex, but I let him after he threatened to cheat. I could see the tension it was causing. And, I didn't want him cheating on me.

So, I just lay there and took it. After four months of no sex he only lasted five minutes anyway.

Pretty soon, I had gotten into a routine that sex time would be the time I would think about anything else. What would I cook for supper? I should clean. What color should I paint the kitchen?

That routine only lasted about three months before I started denying him again. I felt horrible about myself, and frankly stopped caring. It didn't feel good. It was nothing more than a chore I had to do to satisfy my husband. It was no good trying to talk to him about it; I tried and failed.

His cure for being embarrassed about sex, which he explained to me was the issue, was to have more sex. He was completely selfish about sex.

It didn't take long for the fighting to start again. I would deny him, and then we'd fight about it and everything else. The house is a mess, whose job it was to cook every night, and who the inconsiderate jerk was for the night. Until, I would give in and let him have sex with my body.

I became the prude and he became the sex fiend.

A month before our one year anniversary, I found out he was cheating on me.

My fault, right? It was, because I wouldn't have sex with him.

Nevertheless, I gathered up my evidence and took it to the divorce lawyer. By the time he was served with papers, I was moved out and back in the apartment with Dean.

I didn't need a therapist to know that I had to get more comfortable with sex, or probably the next marriage will turn out just the same.

I didn't need a therapist to tell me that I have a lot of issues that need to get worked out. Nor, to tell me that sex wasn't the only issue with my marriage.

First, I decided, I would have to get my confidence back. Lose all the weight that I got during the marriage, and perhaps try to feel sexy.

Dean's cure was an impromptu weekend trip to Las Vegas with his buddies two months after I left my husband.

One girl in a group of seven men. Correction one prude girl with every filter in the world, with seven men who have zero filters whatsoever. Each one of them wanting to help me out with my problem; the apparent sex comfortability problem.

The first thing I found out, was how red my face could go at the slightest comment about sex.

The second, was the guys have a lot of opinions about exactly what is considered sexy or not. And, none of them have issues with a little extra weight.

The third, was that guys are raised completely differently for all matters considered about sex.

By the time we got to the hotel room, the guys had already decided that I was not allowed to make any decisions for myself that weekend.

Apparently, I had been doing everything wrong.

Somehow, Dean had slipped away and was able to purchase me a complete outfit of what I had to wear out dancing.

I was essentially shoved into the shower and told to wash the airport off me, and shave everything except for my head.

For the next two hours, the boys had opinions on everything. Black dress, no stockings, red lipstick to match my heels, straight hair, the sultry smelling perfume, dangly earrings, and no necklace. I even had to match my underwear to their specifications.

Each one of them took all of one minute to get ready. They basically put on different clothes, and sprayed on some cologne.

Then we did something I had never done before; bar hopped.

The night started slow, but soon the guys picked up some strategies. Most of them included just randomly leaving me somewhere.

We'd be dancing and then randomly they'd be gone and some dude would be grinding up against me. They would leave me at the bar, and within no time some guy or another would be buying me a drink. One of the guys would always step in if something was getting too serious, they were always watching, but all of it was definitely a morale booster. With every single one of those boys telling me how sexy and hot I was.

By the fifth bar I didn't even need the boys. I was drunk and I knew I was sexy. I'd wander off and find a boy myself.

Until, I went to the bathroom and threw up. Then I was drunk, sexy, and had alcohol poisoning.

I went over to the table that the boys had sat down at. "I need food. I threw up."

The boys were in a mix of laughing and showing concern. We decided to get out of there. We'd move on to the next bar, and on the way there we'd pick up some food.

I felt good despite having thrown up. It probably was throwing up that made me feel good. Either way, we find a food truck selling the best tacos in the world. I get some food back into my stomach, but the chorus of yawns makes everyone think we should go back to the hotel instead.

It's decided we would walk back to the hotel. It won't be too long of a walk.

"Thanks for tonight. It was fun. I don't think

any of them were quite husband material, but I am pretty sure that half of them were younger than me." I told them.

One of Dean's drunken friends said. "Oh sweetie, we were just trying to get you laid, not trying to get you a husband. This is what you should have been doing in your early twenties. Going out, having fun, experimenting a little. Find out exactly what you like; what you don't like. I mean back then you didn't have to have sex, now you do."

I could hear someone hit him. "Tonight was about confidence, not about having sex. She doesn't have to have sex if she doesn't want to. Though, I would also be willing to help her out with that." He doesn't get to continue as he gets smacked multiple times by, I'm sure, everyone around him. "I was just putting the offer out there."

"If anyone's going to have sex with her it should be Dean." I could hear one distinct smack. I didn't have to turn around to know that it was probably from Dean.

Dean's friends are kind of hot. I could definitely have sex with a couple of them and not even care in the morning.

Once we got back to the hotel, that's apparently exactly what I did.

I remember bits and pieces. What I do remember is hot and sweaty, and amazing. Along with things that I had never done before, including having sex in a stairwell, and immediately having sex with a different guy in the shower.

I then, apparently, decided it was a good idea to go and crawl into bed with Dean; naked. Passing out before anything happened.

I couldn't thank him, internally, enough for running away before I got up the next morning.

Not a single person made any comment about exactly what had happened the night before. No one made a big deal about it.

Like random sex wasn't a big deal. Or, rather sex wasn't a big deal. Not at all the production people made out of losing my virginity after I got married.

It was the first inking I had that maybe sex before or without marriage isn't a big deal.

Well, I mean it is, but maybe not as big of a deal as my parents made it out to be.

All my life, sex was completely taboo. You didn't talk about it.

It was complete blasphemy.

Unthinkable, to even think about thinking about having sex before marriage.

I pledged an oath in front of a congregation of church goers at ten years old. Again, when I was thirteen and obtained a purity ring.

My parents checked in with me to make sure that I knew not to defile myself like that.

Society placed a great importance on it through telling the importance of virgin until marriage.

It was a badge of honour I held high. I actually thought I was better than the girls around me who were losing their virginities to non-serious relationships.

It was made a bigger deal than it had to be for my entire life.

I'm probably not going to have random sex again, but I'm not going to place as much pressure on it. I won't wait until marriage to have sex again.

Hypocrites

My parents were total hypocrites.

Set in my ways, only to have the foundation of my beliefs shaken and crumble underneath me. I rebuild, to have cracks appear. Slipping through the cracks, before patching them up.

Reflection hit me like a midlife crisis. Years of life and living created my own experiences and way of thinking.

Ups and downs. Good and bad. A deep feeling set in, from my reflection, that I could have done better; done more and been more.

It had me thinking about my parents. About everything they taught me before they passed.

I didn't fully understand how hypocritical my parents were with all their rules, until I was thirty two years old and talking with my Aunt Jann.

It all started with a simple question, "Can you tell me more about my parents?"

Rule #1: Always pay with a credit card.

"The real problems started when your parents tried to get an apartment to themselves; they couldn't. And, our parents wouldn't help them.

You don't have a credit history; they would say. You don't exist in the system. You would be too much of a risk. You don't even have collateral.

The same thing happen when your parents went to go get a vehicle; for collateral. You don't have a credit history. They didn't have enough money down.

Finally, your parents convinced your dad's parents to co-sign for both the vehicle and the apartment so they could move out. But, they held it over their head until every cent was paid back. It's why they disappeared from your life.

Your parents made an effort to learn more about credit and decided to get credit cards. They never wanted to be in that mess again.

A good way to build credit is to charge everything to credit cards and pay it off; but the key is to pay if off right away.

They did good for a while; they were even able to buy that house. Unfortunately, it looked like they started spending more than they had; more than they could make. They ended up living a lifestyle on borrowed money."

102

Rule #2: Never leave food on the plate.

"Your grandparents, for a while, were millionaires. When we were young, our parents lost all of it. We had to survive off very little money.

You know, I remember our parents before losing the money. We were allowed to be as picky as we wanted. We got everything we ever wanted. There was always dessert on the table.

But, after they lost the money, we had to cut back. No more dessert, at all. We weren't allowed to be picky anymore. Shiny new toys weren't missed. We cried and threw temper tantrums, of course. But, it was the food that was the most memorable and significant change.

I still can't stomach bologna and mac and cheese. Forget about mushroom soup. I smell it, and I throw up.

If there was nothing but rice on the table, that was what you ate. That was just how it was.

When we did have food, you ate it and you ate all of it. There was no refusing it because you didn't like it. There was no leaving anything behind. You didn't know when you would be able to eat like that again.

Between the four of us, we would eat everything up; not that there was much of anything in the first place."

Rule #3: Never drink alcohol.

"When they were teenagers, your parents drank like fishes.

Well, your mom did until she found out she was pregnant with you. But, then she started up against after you were born.

Your dad drank the whole time.

It stopped when you were three. You got really sick and I had come over by a chance. Both your parents were too drunk to notice how bad you had gotten.

You almost died.

While you were in the hospital for a week, I had an intervention with your parents and got them to work at the problem.

They did pretty good after that; for the most part.

Nothing like almost killing your child to kick alcoholism.

I didn't even know they were drinking again, until the police told me that they caused their own accident by driving drunk.

Your mom was alive when the paramedics came; barely conscious. She was able to tell them that your dad had passed out while he was driving."

Rule #4: Forgive all; life's too short for grudges.

"Your mom did a lot of things that she regretted. There were so many people she hurt when she was drunk.

Quite frankly, she was an ass when she drank. Over confident and zero filter. Didn't care what she did and who she did it to.

She'd go up to a friend's boyfriend and kiss him, among other things, in front of the friend. Or, if someone pissed her off, she'd tell their secrets to the worst possible people.

Once she stopped drinking, she had a lot of people to apologize to.

Not one person, she apologized to, forgave her. She wanted nothing more in the world than to have these people forgive her.

I don't know why, because obviously they weren't very good friends to start with. Not that she was a good friend either; she should have just moved on.

But, I guess your sober mom needed the approval, and needed to be friends with everyone.

She couldn't handle it when people didn't forgive her when she asked for it."

Rule #5: Always help your friends.

"Your parents were the type of people who would give the shirt off their back to help friends and family; anyone really.

It was very admirable of them.

They've helped me with various things over the years. They bought me groceries when I was starving. They helped me move five times.

Your parents were generous people; almost to a fault, but they never saw it that way.

It came down to how others treated them.

Whenever they needed help, people would always seem to disappear.

The reasons felt more like feeble excuses. Ten people would say yes to helping them move, but then everyone would cancel last minute citing some excuse or another.

One would say they forgot and scheduled something else. Another has a hurt back. One would say some reason that wouldn't make sense, like they can't afford to help them move or their diet and exercise regimen wouldn't allow for it.

This happened every time they needed help. No one shared the same sense of ideals.

It hurt them a lot."

Rule #6: Go to University and get a real job.

"When your mom was sixteen, she decided to quit school to help out our parents and get ahead of the game for herself. It wasn't their idea, but she had her mind to it.

She had never gotten good grades and had no idea what she wanted to do. This really didn't open up a lot of jobs for her; all service industry type jobs. Low level and entry jobs at the places that would look beyond a high school dropout.

Your dad graduated high school; barely.

It took a while for a company to pick him up for construction. It was a hard job. He had to deal with a lot of crap. It was good when it was good, but a lot of down time when things were bad. At times he worked crazy hours and a crazy amount of hours. He missed a lot of your life.

They watched all their friends get all these opportunities because they went to university. They had life experiences in university. Then, when they got out, they got amazing jobs. They didn't do back breaking work.

They got the lifestyles, your parents wanted, without resorting to credit cards and debt.

I think every parent wants more for their children. They saw all the missed opportunities and wanted more for you. "

Rule #7: No sex before marriage.

"You probably don't want to hear this, but your mom lost her virginity at sixteen.

It was with the stock boy on her half hour lunch break. There was a string of guys, and one night stands for the next two-three years after that.

Then, there was your dad. After they had a one night stand, he ended up asking your mom out.

About six months later, your parents married: eloped. They didn't have a wedding; they just kind of did it and then told the family and everyone.

Our parents weren't happy. The entire family wasn't happy. She lost friends over it.

Everyone thought she was insane. Everyone voiced it. But, there wasn't anything that they could do about it though, because they were already five months pregnant with you.

There was one friend, her best friend, that went ballistic on her. Told her everything she thought about her lifestyle. It ended the friendship.

A lot of people told her what they thought. It ruined her excitement about being married and pregnant. Hormones and depression.

It got bad."

After so many years I finally understand, at least partially, why my parents had taught me the things they did; had the rules they had.

Everyone has their rules for a reason. Their own rules are made by their experiences from their life.

It's not to say that one person's rules are right or wrong over another person's. It's that not everyone's rules work for everyone. People's experiences are different, and people are different, so they come up with different rules.

Overall, I wouldn't say their rules were completely horrible. They had a good basis for why they had the rules; they had reason.

I just wish my parents hadn't been so concrete, so black and white about everything, while I was growing up.

I wish I had known my parents' reasons earlier. I wish they hadn't kept it a secret.

I wish I had known they were hypocrites earlier. It might have saved me some fumbling around.

Being a hypocrite is part of growing older and experiencing life.

It's taken trial and error however through my experiences; I have made my own set of rules for life.

Rule #1: Many institutions rely on a good credit score. Have a credit card, but make sure you never spend more on your credit card than you can pay off within a month or two.

Rule #2: Don't take more food than you should eat. Try to eat healthy most of the time. You can always leave some for left overs, if there is too much on your plate.

Rule #3: Drink alcohol socially; if you want to. Nothing says you have to or don't have to drink. If you do, you're probably going to drink too much and get a hangover at first; just figure out your limit and try not to get alcohol poisoning. Keep your mind about you, so you aren't regretting anything in the morning. Some people do stupid things while drinking.

Rule #4: Forgive the little things. Life's too short for you to hold grudges because your friend took the last cookie; one time. Forgive, but don't forget. Patterns of small indiscretions can be just as bad as one large betrayal. Don't be afraid to speak up when the person is apologizing, about how they made you feel. There is a line. You can refuse to accept an apology and, if need be, cut ties with them.

Rule #5: Spend time to help people, when you can. If you can't, don't make B.S. excuses. Never lend more money than you're willing to lose. Your friends are not friends if they're only there for the things you give them.

Rule #6: Pay attention in class. Get decent grades. Work as hard as it takes to get what you want out of life. Leave time to relax and have fun, while you are young. Do what you love. If that changes, don't wait years on an improbable chance that it might get better.

Rule #7: No sex, until you've at least graduated high school. Don't be a whore and have sex with a hundred guys. Use protection; only get pregnant by the person you plan on spending the rest of your life with.

My parents were total hypocrites.

Everyone is a hypocrite.

I am a hypocrite.

www.ingramcontent.com/pod-product-compliance
Lightning Source LLC
Chambersburg PA
CBHW020621120726
47905CB00003B/887